The Fox Busters

YEARLING BOOKS/YOUNG YEARLINGS/YEARLING CLASSICS are designed especially to entertain and enlighten young people. Patricia Reilly Giff, consultant to this series, received the bachelor's degree from Marymount College. She holds the master's degree in history from St. John's University, and a Professional Diploma in Reading from Hofstra University. She was a teacher and reading consultant for many years, and is the author of numerous books for young readers.

For a complete listing of all Yearling titles, write to
Dell Readers Service, P.O. Box 1045,
South Holland, IL 60473.

The Fox Busters

DICK KING-SMITH

Illustrated by Jon Miller

A Yearling Book

Published by
Dell Publishing
a division of
Bantam Doubleday Dell Publishing Group, Inc.
666 Fifth Avenue
New York, New York 10103

This work was first published in a hardcover edition in Great Britain by Victor Gollancz Ltd.

The trademark Yearling® is registered in the U.S. Patent and Trademark Office.

ISBN: 0-440-40288-3

Reprinted by arrangement with Delacorte Press

Printed in the United States of America

June 1990

10 9 8 7 6 5 4 3 2

CWO

Contents

The Fox Busters

1
The Ambush

ONE APRIL MORNING, TWELVE PULLETS FROM THE flock at Foxearth Farm were playing an energetic game. They were long-legged, athletic young chickens, still short of the point of their first lay, and thus free to roam all over the place without domestic responsibilities. While foraging together in the barnyard, they had come upon a strange and interesting thing. It was in fact a large brown-and-white-striped peppermint wrapped in a twist of transparent paper; the farmer had dropped the candy from his pocket when he pulled out his handkerchief to blow his nose.

The pullets did not recognize the peppermint as food, but they were attracted by its stripy color and the crackliness of the paper when they pecked at it; anyway they were bursting with energy and just in the mood for a game. One picked it up and dashed off across the yard, pursued by all her friends. All were anxious to grab the trophy, and it was dropped and picked up again, tossed high in the air and caught, or passed from beak to beak to the excited cries of the players. They were jolly girls, healthy girls, hearty girls, and they shouted to each other as they played.

"Chuck it here! Chuck it here! Chuck it! Chuck it! Chuck it!"

"Back! Back! Pass it back!"

"Hard luck! Oh, hard luck!"

"Quick! Quick! Well played, chick!"

How they scuffled and tussled and ran and chased, racing about the yard on their long yellow legs, until at last they tired of their game and, leaving the peppermint in the dust, ran squawking down to the lower yard for a drink at the great stone water-trough.

The surface of the water was green and scummy

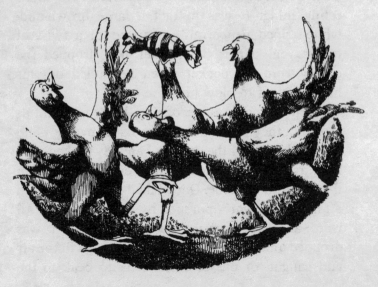

and there was nothing to be seen except a black shiny object about the size of a small prune. This they did not notice.

Some were in the act of bending to scoop up water when, in a dreadful explosion of controlled violence, an old gray-muzzled fox burst up from below the surface.

He took the nearest bird by her downstretched neck in the very instant of his leap from the watery ambush and slipped his wet way out of the yard and off to the woods, to a wild chorus of horror-stricken yells from the survivors.

At the fringe of the boundary trees, the old dog-fox dropped the broken-necked pullet for a moment and shook the water out of his red coat,

shook himself from the point of his long nose to the end of his white-tipped brush.

Turning his head, one forefoot raised, he looked back inscrutably at Foxearth Farm. Then he picked up his prey and was gone.

2
The Extraordinary Hatch

FOXES LIKE ALL KINDS OF THINGS TO EAT, BUT ESPE-
cially they love chickens, and for hundreds and
hundreds of years, the fox has killed and the
chicken has been killed. But one fine day at Foxearth Farm, only a week after one fox had killed
one fowl in the ambush at the great stone trough,
some extraordinary chickens were hatched, who
grew up to do some extraordinary things, as a re-
sult of which the foxes in their lives stopped, one
way or another, loving them altogether.

It all began in a very usual way, when one of
Farmer Farmer's hens went broody. Farmer
Farmer (that was his name, just as there are bakers
called Baker and butchers called Butcher) kept
hens; as well as hens, he kept cows and pigs; and,
as well as cows and pigs, he kept foxes. He didn't in
the least want to keep foxes, of course, but for
many, many years, as the name of the farm tells,
the sandy dells and thick woods of that piece of
country had been the homes of generations of
long-nosed, soft-footed, sharp-eared, red-coated
chicken-lovers. And because Farmer Farmer's
grandfather and father before him had been, as he

was, a little bit slapdash, a little bit happy-go-lucky, a little bit lazy even, generations of Foxearth Farm hens had had to learn the lesson that only the fittest survive. Had they been properly housed or penned, or properly shut up at nights, they might, over the years, have remained fat, dull, comfortable biddies, happy prisoners free from fear.

As it was, Farmer Farmer's chickens had gradually become very different from the usual stupid, squawking, earthbound sort. To begin with, they were all of a dull coloring, brownish or grayish or sandyish, for over the years the white ones and the bright ones and the spotty ones had always been the first to catch the sharp eyes of the chicken lovers on their daylight raids or their night patrols. Next, they were all much longer in the leg than usual, for over the years those who could not run fast enough when the need arose never ran again. Thirdly, they were all quick witted; for over the years those who wandered around corners in a daydream, or went for walks too far from the barnyard, or waited too long before going to bed, never wandered or walked or waited again.

Lastly, and most importantly, the chickens of Foxearth Farm had developed a skill which poultry do not usually possess—they could fly, they could really fly; for over the years flight, real flight, had become the only way to safety from foxes; hiding was no good, running was no good, nor was the sort of short-range, low-altitude, frantic fluttering which is all a hen can usually manage.

The Foxearth birds could actually remain airborne for long distances and could easily reach quite useful heights such as, for example, the thirty-foot-high top of the stack of hay bales in Farmer Farmer's Dutch barn, up to which there flew, with strong confident beats of her long graceful wings, the dullest-brown, longest-legged, sharpest-witted hen of them all. After a quick and careful look all around, she settled herself in a comfortable rounded gap between two bales.

Here was her nest containing eleven eggs, and she proceeded to lay a twelfth. In three weeks' time a dozen ordinary brownish middle-sized eggs would, with luck, hatch out. They did. But what an extraordinary hatch it was.

3
The Three Sisters

AT FIRST THE TWELVE NEWBORN CHICKS, ALL ABOUT
the color of a soldier's khaki shirt, seemed just another family to their mother, whose name was
Spillers. It should be explained that one of the ad-
vantages the high intelligence of the Foxearth
fowls gave them was an ability to notice and eventually to read the many and varied pieces of writing to be found about the farm and its yards and
buildings and fields. While addressing each other
in Hennish, they used these farm words or parts of
sentences—for some notices, for instance, were too
long to be used as a whole—as names for themselves, finding them as they did on cake sacks and
meal sacks and fertilizer bags, on tractor name-
plates and pieces of farm machinery and notice
boards.

Thus you might see scratching about the barnyard in company Fisons and Alfa-Laval, Fordson
and Leyland, or Trespassers and Beware Of.
Fullwood and International Harvester might sit
companionably in adjoining nests, or David Brown
and John Deere crow upon the same fence. Punctu-
ation of course meant nothing to the birds, so that

there were several hens—and cockerels, for the names were used equally for males or females—called Icky, this being their interpretation of the label ICI upon many polyethylene sacks.

The husband of this particular Spillers, and thus the father of the newborn twelve, was an especially gifted rooster bearing the noble old name of Massey-Harris; he was gifted, that is to say, in the hard-won Foxearth tradition of being able to avoid or outwit the long-nosed chicken-lovers, and thus to survive and to breed survivors in his own image. Like his wife Spillers, he possessed in a high degree all that was best in a Foxearth fowl. He stood tall and poised on long strong legs; on each side of a constantly turning watchful head were large, far-seeing eyes; and the dull brown flight feathers of his powerful wings, and the plumes of his great tail which balanced him when he flew, were the longest and strongest of the flock.

In character, curiously, husband and wife were not alike. He was impulsive and bold, she thoughtful and cautious; he greeted the world with a blustering shout, she kept her counsel; he was a public and she a private person.

They were unalike, too, in their habits; for example, one of the feedstuffs which Farmer Farmer used for his cattle was a supply of brewers' wet grains which was brought by truck and unloaded in a great heap; these grains were the residue from the malting barley which the brewers used to make beer, and most of the adult males of the flock enjoyed a cropful of the damp brown stuff, at midday or in the evening. It made them noisier, and friendlier—or sometimes much less friendly—than they normally were; it made them feel confident and superior; it took away their worries; and it gave them an excuse to get away from their loving wives for a while—for on the whole hens were not welcome at the grain heap—and from tiresome nestside duties and the constant hen parties with their unending chat about incubation and hatching and chick rearing. In short, it made them feel birds of a feather, and most days Massey-Harris would say to his wife, "Er, just going to pop down for a grain or two with the boys, dear. Just half a cropful. Bit peckish. Won't be late."

But he nearly always was and sometimes, if too loud or too boastful, felt the lash of his lady's tongue.

Spillers's life, by contrast, revolved around her current family. Her chicks were to her all important, she was intensely nest proud, and she was extremely neat in her person with never a feather out of place. With words she was sparing, but what she said was always to the point, and when she made a decision or gave an order, nobody questioned it. Sizing up this prim, competent, cool individual, no one would have guessed how she adored her big bluff husband, with his high-flown talk and his happy-go-lucky ways.

In their habits of speech, too, they were quite different. With her children Spillers was much given to the use of hatchphrases, repeated over the years to each of her many broods so that they became part of the Hennish language. Stubborn chicks were told "Don't-Care was made to care," nervous chicks that "There's no such words as *can't*," overexcited chicks that "It'll all end in tears." Greedy chicks were told not to speak with their crops full and chicks who used naughty words were warned that they would have their beaks washed out with saddle soap. Wastefulness was not encouraged ("There's many a starving sparrow would be grateful for that grain of wheat"), and Spillers's chicks had always to eat up their corn before they were allowed their pellets.

Not surprisingly, one of her favorite sayings was "Mother knows best."

Massey-Harris also was predictable in the things he said, but his observations tended to be much more sweeping and less practical than his wife's. If a young Foxearth cockerel was heard to remark, for instance, that the only good fox was a dead fox, you could be sure he was one of Massey-Harris's boys, though some of the father's favorite phrases were less acceptable to the sons; he tended to criticize their flying abilities ("Wings aren't what they used to be"), their manners ("I always called *my* father 'Sir' "), and their appearance ("The scruffy long-feathered young chaps of today"). He could be very pompous, and he had a good opinion of himself; for example he always used himself as a yardstick when handing out praise for good behavior or effort, and many a Massey-Harris chick would say jokingly—out of father's hearing—"Couldn't have done better myself."

On this particular hatchday, Massey-Harris took off from the sack platform of the big red combine harvester after which he was named, and flew up to the height of Spillers's nest. Here he hovered hawklike, another skill which Farmer Farmer's poultry had perfected, and cried to his wife, "What luck?"

"Twelve out of twelve, dear," she replied, and Massey-Harris, with a shout of "Full marks!" performed a victory roll above the roof of the Dutch barn before gliding to the nest to inspect his latest children. The mother hen stood up and moved aside.

"I must say," she said with a sigh of satisfaction, "I do so like to see a hundred percent hatch. I find it very upsetting when a chick is too weak to get out, or worse, when an egg has no chick in it."

"Can't remember that happening in any clutch of yours, old lady," said Massey-Harris, loudly, because he often spoke at the top of his voice, and proudly, because he was sure there wasn't another hen in the flock as clean and neat a nestwife as his Spillers. Why, already the mess of broken eggshells had been scratched to one side of the beautifully made, saucer-shaped nest, and the nestlings were arranged neatly, ready for their father's inspection. As always, he forgot his strong male image as he looked down at the twelve round scraps of yellow fluff.

"What are little pullets made of?" he said softly. "Larvae and lice and all things nice. That's what little pullets are made of." And then, "What are little cockerels made of? Slugs and snails and pollywogs' tails. That's what little cockerels are made of."

Raising his voice to its usual brassy pitch, he continued, "Jolly good strong-looking lot, m'dear. Couldn't have done better—er, that is, I mean, all credit to you. You must be glad it's all over."

"Yes, I am," said the hen. "Three weeks seems a

long time when you're sitting still. Just think, in another three weeks they'll be starting to fly."

No sooner were the words out of her beak than the most extraordinary thing happened. One of the new-hatched babies stood up in the nest, took two or three tiny steps clear of its brothers and sisters —and flew! Admittedly it was no great flight, no more than a couple of feet up into the air, a level course over the length of half a dozen hay-bales, and a rather untidy landing in the center of the stack. But the hour-old chick was unmistakably flying; and in a moment it made the return flight, to land, more smoothly this time, in the nest.

Mother and father gazed open-beaked at this marvel.

"Do you see," said Spillers, examining the tiny thing carefully, "its wings are much more developed than I'd have believed possible."

"They are, they are," said Massey-Harris, "they're much larger and longer than usual."

"And look," went on Spillers, "they haven't got down on them like ordinary day-olds, they've got minute formed flight-feathers."

The parents examined the other occupants of the nest with great and growing excitement and found that though nine of the hatch seemed no different from normal, active, advanced Foxearth chicks, there were two others who, like the first wonder-chick, had this strange wing-development. They, too, perhaps not quite as strongly as the first but nonetheless remarkably, made short return flights over the bales of hay.

As the weeks went by and the other nine chicks, like all that curious flock, began to fly down to the ground to feed and forage and then back up to the top of the barn as easily as a pack of sparrows, so the great gifts of the first three fliers became more apparent. They could fly faster, higher, and farther than their nest mates; and soon, comparing the development of combs and the set of tails, Spillers and Massey-Harris realized that of their twelve chicks nine were little cockerels and three, the gifted three, were little pullets.

These were the three sisters, tiny as yet, insignificant now, but already showing amazing powers, who were to become a legend to future generations

at Foxearth Farm. The deeds which they were yet to perform would be told, in years to come, by every hen to every brood of chicks. More, they would be told by every vixen to every litter of fox cubs in the sandy dells and thick woods of that piece of country. These were the Fox Busters.

4
The Other Side

WHILE ALL THIS WAS HAPPENING, THE LIVES OF THE foxes went on as usual. They fed themselves and their cubs on the best they could find—which nowadays was seldom chicken. And though the foxes fared well enough, nevertheless they hankered after a taste of freshly caught poultry; and they were aware of the problems facing them in satisfying this longing. To begin with, the other farmers in the district kept their hens in deep-litter houses or in battery sheds and did not, unlike Farmer Farmer, give a fox much chance. And secondly, any chances that were offered at Foxearth Farm were becoming increasingly slim, due of course to the flock's ability to take to the air.

So the chicken-loving long-noses began to increase their daylight raids and night patrols and, as will happen if you try something often enough, occasionally had some luck. However well the Foxearth fowls might fly by day, they still had to eat and drink; and though many took water from the gutters on the buildings, they still had to come to earth for grain or mash or pellets.

Thus an elderly hen named Gascoigne was

snapped up at her breakfast by a long-nose who had slipped into the yard with the last of the night, and had hidden himself in a bed of wild garlic that bordered the part of the yard where Farmer Farmer usually threw down some corn; the fox was of course risking the attentions of the farm dogs, but the smell of the garlic masked even his sharp scent.

One of the Fordsons delayed a second too long, and was pulled down at takeoff by a particularly speedy young dog fox; and even at night, once, a slim and very active vixen managed to climb to the top of a huge heap of broken straw-bales and kill an Alfa-Laval who was brooding seven chicks; the vixen ate the chicks in seven gulps and slid down the stack and away with the hen slung over her shoulder.

But on the whole the many foxes which the farmer unwillingly kept upon his land fared very badly indeed with regard to the food which they loved best; most of the younger ones had never tasted chicken and listened, green eyed and slobber chopped, to the stories which some of the elders of the tribe would tell, stories handed down from their great-great-grandfathers, stories of the days long ago when Foxearth fowls were as easy meat as any others; then a fox could dance into a bunch of shining-white, short-legged, earthbound hens, twisting off a dozen silly heads as he went and leaving the bodies bouncing and fluttering their last, and away—just for the fun of it! He wouldn't even bother to take one with him, the elders said—he would probably have eaten so much chicken recently as to be sick of it. "Sick of it!" cried a youngster. "Just imagine!"

"Just imagine hens that couldn't fly!" cried another. "Why, killing them would be cubs' play."

"Easy as kiss your paw," said an old vixen.

"You can't even get a meal of eggs or chicks nowadays," said another graymuzzle with a sigh. "These wretched flying fowls, they all nest high."

"Eggs. Eggs. Eggs," intoned one. "Crack 'em up and suck 'em down."

"Chicks. Little chicks," moaned another. "Lovely soft warm little mouthfuls."

"Tasty heads," groaned a third. "Crunch them. Munch them."

Even the oldest fox broke silence at last.

"The breast meat," he said very softly, "thick, juicy slices of breast meat. The breast meat is the best meat."

At the end of the day, maddened by these lip-licking stories and driven by sheer longing to sample this heavenly food of which their seniors spoke, a group of young, tough, and active foxes determined to *do* something about it. There were four of them, two brothers and two sisters from a litter, whose sire was the most cunning and whose dam was the swiftest of all the foxes in the sandy dells and thick woods of that piece of country. And, at

about the same time that the three sisters from the extraordinary hatch were four months old, these young foxes put their long noses together and began to make plans.

5
The Aeronauts

THE NAMING OF YOUNG CHICKS WAS TRADITIONALLY, for the Foxearth flock, a serious business, demanding much thought and a good deal of close observation by mothers and fathers in their daily movements about the farm. Had Farmer Farmer, for instance, bought any new piece of machinery which might bear an interesting name hitherto unknown? Had he changed his brand of dairy cake, or stocked up with a fresh kind of fertilizer, or put up any new notices?

Spillers and Massey-Harris had given a lot of attention to the choice of names for their latest brood; or more truthfully, they had each privately decided that any good, well-respected name would do for the little cockerels—Bamford, Icky, Crosfield, Beware Of—but that the three pullets, by virtue of their exceptional abilities, deserved names never before used, names which would stand out as different, just as the three sisters themselves were extraordinary.

Thus it was with keen pleasure that Massey-Harris made just the required discovery one bright morning. Rising early, at his own crow that is, he

flew from his special roosting place in the middle
of the central A-frame high in the lofty roof of the
great barn, through the tall open double doors, and
over the jumble of farm buildings toward a single
Scots pine which stood in the home paddock. It
was from the top branches of this old and totally
foxproof tree that he was accustomed to shout
each morning's defiance at long-noses far and
near, and to preen his feathers, and to scan the
surrounding acres for any signs of danger.

On this particular morning, however, his flight
path taking him as it always did over a thick patch
of nettles midway between the boundary hedge
and the pine, his sharp eye saw unaccustomed
movement among the tall stinging plants; and, hovering like a kestrel ten feet above the ground, Massey-Harris saw a litter of young rabbits vanish in
sudden fright beneath a long rusty object; he had
not previously noticed this object because he had
never happened to hover just there before. Made
bold by the presence aboveground of the rabbits,
which more or less guaranteed the absence of a
fox, for the whole nettle patch was no bigger than a
billiard table, he dropped gently on to the rusty
thing, and found himself perched upon the beam
of an old and long-discarded horse plow.

By chance, the metal label carrying the name of
the makers was fixed to the implement at the exact
spot on which he had pitched. Quickly, for it wasn't
a place to hang about in, the big rooster pecked
with his strong beak at the rust and mud which

23

covered the nameplate and soon revealed some writing.

At first he could make no sense of it, but then he

realized that from his perch the writing was upside down, and hopped off, down into the deep nettle bed. He turned and confronted the words. RAN-SOME, SIMS & JEFFERIES, the label read, and in a flash he realized that these names, never before used in the Foxearth flock, were heaven sent—perhaps by Chanticleer, great god of domestic fowls—for the express benefit of the three talented pullets. With a great cry of triumph which sounded something like "Eureka!" Massey-Harris shot up into the air like a jump jet, and beat strongly away to tell his mate the news.

Spillers clucked the names over to herself several times.

"Yes. I like them," she said. "What's more," she continued, "they fit each of them rather neatly."

"I don't follow," said Massey-Harris.

"Well," she said, "the one that flew first on their hatchday—she's the fastest and strongest flier of the three and, when they play, she's always the ringleader. *R* for ringleader, *R* for Ransome. And one of the other two seems very sensible and serious-minded, while the other is more jolly, fond of a joke. *S* for sensible, *S* for Sims, *J* for jolly, *J* for Jefferies. Get it?"

"Oh, very good, very good!" cried Massey-Harris. "Couldn't have done better myself."

"No," said Spillers.

So the three hitherto nameless pullets—the cockerels had already been named—were told of their titles. The honor and privilege of being the first owners of such handsome names excited Ransome, Sims, and Jefferies very much, and in their pleasure and pride they proceeded to treat their parents to a magnificent display of aerobatics such as only they, with their fantastic wing development, were able to perform.

First, they took off together from the ridgepole of the farmhouse, where they had chanced to be at the time of their father's return, and, in tight for-

25

mation, made a high-speed circuit of the farmyard. Then, wing tip to wing tip, they flew in at one window of the milking parlor and out at the other, frightening the four Friesians who were being milked at the time so that they roared and jumped and kicked off the units. Next, with Farmer Farmer's yells of anger following them, they turned tightly around the corner of the collecting yard, to the surprise and consternation of the rest of the dairy herd.

They set course for the farrowing house and flashed down its length with the speed of three wood pigeons, to the sound of a babel of terrified squeals and furious grunts.

Emerging in line ahead now, Ransome leading, then Sims, then Jefferies, they swept twice through the upper part of the Dutch barn, looping up over the roof in a perfect display of upside-down flight before the reentry.

Then, in a V-formation—Ransome half a length

ahead of the other two—they dived down and skimmed the surface of the duck pond, wheeled in a dizzy upward spiral around and around the walls of the tall grain silo, and, spiraling still, like gulls in a thermal, climbed and climbed until, to the watchers on the roof, they were no more than three tiny specks in the clear blue sky.

Now came the climax of the show. Ransome, Sims, and Jefferies leveled off at a thousand feet and then suddenly, dramatically, peeled off at precise intervals into an almost vertical dive, like the stoop of three great peregrine falcons. Sharp beaks clamped shut, long necks outstretched, powerful wings clamped to their sides, strong legs retracted, they fell earthward.

Their target was a chance one; one of the farm dogs, minding his own business, was unconcernedly trotting home across the paddock and it was his misfortune that his black-and-white shape set against the green background of the field had caught the eyes of the terrible three.

The watchers on the farmhouse roof saw him stop, look skyward, and then press himself down in the grass with a horrified howl as in turn Ransome, Sims, and Jefferies, braking with suddenly spread wings, flattened out and skimmed with whistling pinions a mere foot or two above his cringing shape.

Sensible Sims broke off the engagement and flew soberly to hover over the farmhouse, and then volplaned gently down to a perfect two-point landing among the family upon the roof.

Jefferies the joker rolled like a raven as she peeled off, and turned a couple of quick somersaults in the air before flopping down amid her brothers with a gobble of chuckles and cackles at the fun of the whole thing.

But Ransome the ringleader wasn't finished yet. Whizzing over the target, she had hurled herself up to loop an enormous loop, sixty or seventy feet high at its top, and, curling down, had come out of it exactly on the line of the terrified collie, who was by now streaking for the safety of his kennel. Fast as he ran, she flew faster. At the gate, she was fifty yards behind him. By the great stone trough in the lower yard, thirty. At the Dutch barn at the top of the barnyard, ten. And as he hurled himself into the straw-filled blackness of his wooden kennel, her beak tweaked the tip of his outstretched plumy tail.

Majestically, with complete mastery of the air, Ransome wheeled away, swept upward, circled, side-slipped, swooped, and finally spread her great wings in a perfect eagle's glide to the ridgepole of the farmhouse. Light as one of her own feathers, she pitched exactly between her proud silent mother and her proud loud father.

"Oh, well done!" he shouted. "Well done, Ransome! Well done, all three of you! Fantastic! Fabulous! Faultless!" and to his wife, "What a display, my dear! Couldn't have done better myself!"

28

"No," said Spillers.

"I specially liked the way they dived on that dog," roared Massey-Harris.

"Yes," said Spillers thoughtfully. "Just suppose that had been a long-nose."

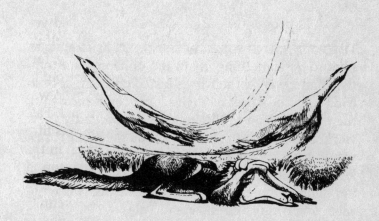

6
The Great Raid *(The Plan)*

THE FOUR YOUNG FOXES, DETERMINED, AS HAS BEEN said, to *do* something about the unhappy fact that they had never in their lives tasted chicken, at first tried such measures as their elders could have told them would lead to little success. Admittedly they worked harder at the business than the older foxes would have bothered to do; the latter were more or less resigned to the fact that Foxearth fowls were too difficult a prey, and contented themselves with rabbits and rats and mice and voles.

At first, the four were tireless in their efforts. They hung about the barnyard every night, on silent patrol or in stealthy ambush, refusing other possible victims in their single-minded resolve to kill poultry. But they drew a blank, for the flock was alarmed by this regular rather than occasional threat from the long-noses, and roosted in the highest and safest places.

The four raiders also made daylight sorties, coming singly or in pairs in sudden swift rushes. Once they even galloped in, four abreast, yapping and snarling, risking the farm dogs and the farmer's gun in an effort to panic the flock, but they soon learned that the flying skills of both adults and growing youngsters were such as to make their best efforts of no use. The baby chicks were of course all hatched in high places.

At last, after some weeks of fruitless endeavour, including an unsuccessful attempt to copy the trick of the old underwater ambusher, the four young foxes came to the conclusion that some hard thinking and precise planning were needed. One evening they were lying in a grassy hollow, scratching their fleas and yawning after a nap, when one sat up and said, "Simple question. Why is it that we can't catch a Foxearth fowl?"

"Well, that's obvious," replied his brother, "they fly too well."

"Why do they?"

"Because they've got blooming great wings, of course. Why do you ask such silly questions?"

"Sorry," said the first speaker, "I'm just trying like mad to think of some way in which we can outwit them."

While the brothers had been talking, the two vixens listened. Then suddenly both sat bolt upright, ears pricked, green eyes alight, staring at each other.

"Suppose," said one of them, "just suppose . . . that they couldn't fly, or at any rate couldn't fly far, or up to any height?"

"Yes," said her sister, jumping to her feet, "so that the four of us could spring up at them, say five or

six feet—we can all do that—and fluster them, and tire them out, and pull them down . . ."

"And eat 'em and eat 'em and eat 'em!" barked the two sisters together at the tops of their voices.

"But where could we possibly do that?" cried the two dog foxes, catching their sisters' enthusiasm.

"Why, the fruit pen, of course!" shouted the vixens, and all four began to yap as loudly as they could, "The fruit pen! The fruit pen! The fruit pen!" so loudly in fact that the distant fowls, who were beginning to fly up to their night roosts, paused and cocked their heads and listened in puzzlement to this strange long-nose chorus.

Having realized at last the first essential for success, the raiders now began to plan in earnest; and

this, after long, excited deliberation, was their detailed scheme. Farmer Farmer had, at the side of the farmhouse, a walled garden, the gate of which he had long since ceased troubling to shut against his birds, since these could all fly with ease over the high walls and sample his vegetables as they wished.

Within the garden, however, was a fruit pen, perhaps the size of a largish living room and completely poultry proof, in which the farmer grew the strawberries of which he was particularly fond. The pen was made of stout larch poles between which was stretched chicken wire of too small a mesh to admit even a sparrow; it was roofed with the same, and had a well-fitted wire door. Farmer

33

Farmer, like his forebears, was a small man, so the pen was no more than five and a half feet in height. It was, the raiders had realized, the perfect trap.

There were three main problems confronting them. First, they had to lure the fowls into the garden and then into the fruit pen; second, they had to keep them there long enough to kill as many as possible, for though they realized that they would only be able to carry away one each, yet their lack of success so far had made them so bitterly angry that they would cheerfully have slaughtered every bird in the flock, cockerel, pullet, and chick; and third, they must be able to make good their own escape after the killing. With these considerations in mind, the four young foxes laid their plans with the utmost care, and decided to put them into execution in one week's time.

7

The Great Raid
(The Execution)

SEVEN DAYS LATER, THE FOXEARTH FLOCK AWOKE AT the crowing of Massey-Harris and his fellow roosters; they stretched and preened themselves, preparing for a little early-morning foraging to keep off the pangs of hunger until the farmer, his milking finished, should come to scatter their corn and pellets.

No fowl had fallen to the long-noses for some time, and they had been almost amused at the vain efforts of the four young foxes, so obviously inexperienced and unsuccessful. The Foxearth flock was perhaps a little overconfident, and when a dozen or so of them flew down from their night roosts and pitched on a patch of ground quite near the gate of the walled garden, they did not react as true Foxearthers should have done to the sight of several large strawberries lying on the ground. They reacted, that is, not with caution, but with careless greed.

All Foxearth fowls were of course not equal. Some, due both to their family background and a lack of first-class training, were less thoughtful, less cautious, and thus destined to be less long lived than others; and it happened that this particular group contained a number who might justly have been called a little feather brained. These—there were six of them—set off upon the trail of strawberries which led toward the gate of the walled garden, with such unthinking excitement that they drew their more sensible companions with them; and indeed soon, attracted by cackles of pleasure and surprise, more of the flock came flying toward the gate and landed to follow the leaders.

The trail of dropped strawberries—one every yard or so, enough to keep the greedy ones rushing forward, pulling the rest behind them—led from the gate along a box-edged path directly to the wire door of the fruit pen. And when the leaders reached this door, they found what they had never found before—that it was wide open!

The four foxes, their plans as well laid as they could contrive, had slipped into the farmyard at dead of night. They came in upwind, moving very slowly and stealthily, intent upon disturbing no one. The garden gate was, as usual, open, and four low shadows floated along the shrubbery-edged path to the door of the fruit pen.

One of the two vixens stood upon her hind legs, and after several attempts successfully used her long nose to undo the hook-and-eye catch, and a paw to pull the door open. Next, the four began methodically to select, by the light of a fitful moon, the largest strawberries. One by one, carrying a berry at a time in their mouths, they laid the trail.

Now, four hours later, they were lying in complete concealment. The farmer had a greenhouse at one side of the walled garden, behind which stood an old heavy wooden table once used in his grandfather's kitchen and now covered with and flanked by many piles of clay flower pots of all shapes and sizes. Underneath this table lay the four raiders. A strong night breeze had blown away the sharp smell of fox from the fruit pen, and now the morning air was still and scentless. Pressed tensely to the ground, they watched the scavenging leaders reach the fruit-pen door.

Here the fowls did hesitate; the sight of the open door when they knew to a bird that this particular one had always been shut made them momentarily suspicious. But drawn by their greed at the view of the strawberry bed spread out before them, and urged on by the press behind them, the leaders moved into the pen and began to gobble up the juicy fruit.

An old Ferguson cackled shrilly with glee at the sight of such a feast. "Come on in, it's lovely!" she cried, and soon there were twenty-five or so hens and half a dozen roosters, perhaps a quarter of the whole flock, eagerly pecking and swallowing inside the pen.

With the exception of hens who were brooding eggs, almost all the rest of the Foxearth flock, including, of course, Massey-Harris and Spillers and their twelve children, had flown to find out the cause of all the excitement, and were perched around the walls of the garden like spectators at a football match.

All were undecided what to do, their natural caution weakened by the hubbub, and some were in the act of dropping down to join in the game when suddenly, silently, swiftly, the foxes raced out from the back of the greenhouse.

One dog fox ran to the garden gate to act as lookout for farmer and dogs and the other three dashed straight for the fruit pen, the two vixens bursting in upon the feasters while their second brother crouched in the mouth of the pen's door, ready to deal with would-be escapers.

What happened now was truly terrible. It was beyond the wildest dreams of the hunters and the most ghastly nightmares of the victims. Caught in the narrow confines of the perfect trap and attacked by what seemed like a host of snapping, snarling, leaping demons, the wretched strawberry pickers lost every vestige of their hard-won sense and, their great powers of flight denied them, fluttered and blundered their way into the netting, into each other, into the very jaws of the killers.

In three minutes, before the horrified gaze of the watchers on the wall, the fruit pen was littered with dead or dying chickens, the gate guard had

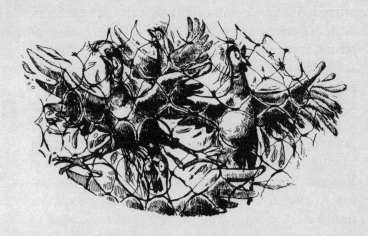

given one sharp bark of warning and had dashed for the pen to claim his share, and then all four foxes, red heads held high against the weight of their prizes, were out of the fruit pen, out of the garden, out of the farmyard, and away, before the farmer from his milking and the dogs from their kennels were halfway to the scene of slaughter.

And what a scene it was. Sainsbury and Silcocks, Bamford and Kidd, old Ferguson and young Dunlop, noble Allis-Chalmers and mighty Minneapolis-Moline, Thornber and Howard, Rice and Lister, Beware Of, Simplex and Claas and many, many more lay in a sea of dull-brown feathers amid the flattened strawberry bed, the bright color of its fruit now stained by splashes of a darker red.

As the four grim raiders crossed the home paddock with their booty, one last strange incident occurred. At some common impulse, Ransome, Sims, and Jefferies, who had been watching horror struck from the garden wall, took off, impelled by some mixture of terror and fury, and flew in tight formation after the cantering foxes, and dived despairingly upon them.

And as they dived, because they were now at the point of lay and in the excess of their frenzy, an egg burst out from one of them (legend says it was Ransome) and smashed upon the rump of the last fox to gain the edge of the bordering wood. The four killers disappeared, the three sisters came to their senses and wheeled back to the farm, and the farmer groaned and cursed as he stood among his growling dogs in his blood-soaked strawberry bed. The great raid was over.

8
The Postmortem

It was the evening of the same day. In the sandy dells and thick woods of that piece of country there was great joy as the news of the massacre spread among the long-noses. Long faces split in ugly grins and long tongues lolled out in amusement at the thought that at last the so clever, high-flown, uncatchable Foxearth flock had been outmaneuvered, deceived, fooled—in a word, had been foxed! Even the most cynical of the elders, as they listened to the raiders' report and heard their rapturous comments on their first meal of chicken, drooled with jealousy and sighed for the days of their great-great-grandfathers.

"Tell us again," said a graying old vixen. "Were they fat? Were they juicy?" and as she spoke the spittle ran out of the corners of her mouth.

"Juicy, certainly," replied one of the four, belching gently, "but not exactly fat. Good lean meat. Excellent flavor," and he licked his chops in contentment while the listeners licked theirs in envy.

"Yes," he went on. "You can keep your rabbits."

"And your rats and mice," said the second one.

"And your voles and shrews," said the third.

"And your beetles and grubs," sniggered the last.

"In fact," said the four with one voice, "we love chicken."

Nevertheless, full bellied as they were—for they had cracked up every last little bone of their prizes —and puffed up as they were with pride at their success, the killers were still shrewd enough to have already realized that such a game could not be played twice. They guessed that no fowl would enter the walled garden for a long time, let alone the fruit pen; and they were also certain that any fox foolish enough to visit the farm in the near future would face patrolling dogs and the flash and roar of Farmer Farmer's gun. They licked their chops, dreamed their dreams, and bided their time.

As for the flock, they were shocked and stunned. They could not believe that such a terrible thing had happened. To think that thirty of their number should have died in just three minutes!

As night fell, the ridgepoles of the farmhouse and of every farm building were crowded with fowls, for with the picture of the fruit pen horribly clear in their minds, none could bear the thought of roosting in any sort of confined space.

To a bird, they were hypnotized by the thought of the four killers, whose exploits of the morning had given them the status of werefoxes, possessed of magic powers. Even the great stone trough story, which had become a stock cautionary tale told by

mothers to careless chicks, paled into insignificance beside this horror.

Though they were perched thirty or forty feet above ground, the fowls expected to see at any moment dark shapes climbing up an ivied wall or swarming up a drainpipe. That night the flock had little sleep.

Sleepless also, the farmer moved restlessly in his bed. Even while hot plans of revenge filled his mind, he knew that they would probably be vain. There were so many foxes, so skilled in avoiding gins and wires, in detecting poison baits, in decamping to reserve dens before the threat of gassing, in keeping out of range of the gun. He knew he must eventually resign himself to the thought that the morning's massacre had been a freakish, thousand-to-one-against chance, and that in the future, as in the past, the flock would manage to keep clear of trouble through their powers of flight.

Tomorrow he would pluck and dress the dead which he had collected and hung in his larder; at any rate there would be plenty of chicken in the deepfreeze for some time to come.

His strawberry bed was ruined, of course; this had made him almost as angry as the death of so many of his fowls. What had possessed him, he thought angrily, to be so careless as to leave the door of the fruit pen open? In their kennels, the farm collies whined uneasily, conscious of duty left undone.

Next morning, however, the sun shone as

brightly as ever, and the survivors, as survivors do, ate their breakfasts with appetite and were glad to be alive. Of course, the Foxearth fowls could not simply dismiss the raid from their minds, like ordinary silly farmyard birds, or even forget already that it had ever happened, as lesser poultry would have done. But their attitude was still a purely defensive one of self-preservation and of resignation to what was for them an age-old and indisputable fact—that foxes, because they love chickens, and because they have sharp teeth and strong jaws, have always killed and will always kill them; that there is no means of stopping this; and that all any fowl can do is keep out of the way. Not one of them had ever thought of carrying the fight to the enemy —till now. It happened like this.

Spillers, her mate, and her twelve children, their crops filled, were sitting and preening in the sunshine, perched in a row on the roof of the Dutch barn. Their backs were turned to the walled garden but they were willing, for all that, to face facts. They were thinking that though none of the flock would ever fall into that particular trap again and though the long-noses might well have the wit to keep away for a while for fear of reprisals, nevertheless there would be more raids to come; these, though unlikely to be as successful as the massacre of the fruit pen, would still probably be more dangerous and frequent than of old. Yet their only refuge was in flight.

Massey-Harris spoke their joint thoughts aloud.

"Chickens have always known," he said with a sigh, "that their only safety lay in flight."

Spillers thoughtfully drew a wing feather through her bill and repeated the last three words of her husband's remark to herself in an undertone. "Lay in flight . . . lay in flight," she murmured, and then she said, addressing herself to Ransome, Sims, and Jefferies, "That was an extraordinary thing that happened when you brave girls were chasing those long-noses over the paddock, wasn't it? We saw it from the top of the garden wall." And without waiting for an answer she said to Massey-Harris, "Do you remember the aerobatic display the girls gave us on their naming day?"

Less quick witted than his wife, the big rooster merely replied, "Of course I do. That *was* something to crow about."

"You miss my point," said Spillers impatiently. "Look at it like this. One. The girls fly down and terrify an animal. Right? It happens to be a dog. Two. The girls fly at another animal—it happens to be a long-nose—and actually hit it, with an object. Right?"

"Which," said Massey-Harris sourly, feeling himself henpecked, "happened to be an egg, and happened to smash, and no doubt the long-nose happened to lick it off his bottom with great enjoyment when he got home."

"But the facts are," persisted his wife, "that we have three brave daughters who can fly better than any fowl ever did, and who can—at least one has and I don't see why the other two shouldn't—'lay in flight.' Put all that together, and if only there was some way to make the eggs more dangerous, we could organize our own raid—against the long-noses."

"Are you telling me," said Massey-Harris slowly, "that chickens could . . . attack . . . foxes, could hurt them, perhaps even . . . kill them?"

"Right," said Spillers.

"Right," said Ransome, Sims, and Jefferies with one voice.

"Only the one thing to solve," said Spillers, "and that's how can an egg be made to hurt a fox?"

"Well, I must say," said Massey-Harris admiringly, "you really are a hard-boiled lot."

9
The Bombing Range

THERE WERE A NUMBER OF WORDS NOT NORMALLY used in polite conversation within the flock. These were almost without exception terms relating to the shameful uses to which people put the chicken and its product, the egg. Verbs like *to roast, to grill,* or *to fricassee,* nouns like *giblets, livers,* and the disgusting *omelette,* adjectives such as *fried, scrambled, baked, poached,* and *Scotch*—all these came under the general heading of "fowl language," and were only made use of very occasionally in times of stress.

So the family's first reaction to Massey-Harris's words was one of raised combs and embarrassed side glances. But in a moment the three brainy sisters looked at each other and their beaks fell open in surprise as the same thought struck them simultaneously.

"Hard . . . er," they said hesitantly, and then, compelling themselves, "hard boiled? Wouldn't that mean that, er, in the case of eggs, um, they, well, finish up . . . sort of not as breakable as usual?" They paused and looked at their mother.

"Cluck cluck," said Spillers testily, "do we really

have to discuss the revolting things that go on in people's kitchens?"

"But do you know the answer, Mother?" chipped in the boldest of the young cockerels. "I mean," he went on, blushing to the roots of his comb and wattles, "how *do* they hard-boil an egg?"

"Apparently," replied Spillers with an expression of extreme distaste upon her face, "the egg is placed in some kind of pot full of water, which is then put on a fire or some other source of heat and . . ." she hesitated ". . . boiled"—she shuddered—"for a long time."

"So the egg gets very hard?" said the young cockerel.

"I believe so," replied his mother. "My old Granny Goodyear once told me something about all this awful sort of business. She was very inquisitive and thick skinned as a pullet, and used to sit on an apple branch outside the kitchen window and watch."

Nobody spoke for a long time. They all sat, shaking their heads and scratching meditatively at the sides of their faces, while they thought about what had been said. At last Massey-Harris spoke.

"Well, that's all very fine and large," he said. "I see what the girls are getting at—hard eggs would make good missiles—but as for all this business of pots of water and fires . . . well, that's got me fox —I mean, that's got me puzzled."

It was Spillers, as usual, with her hard common

sense, who put her claw on the nub of the problem. "Look," she said, "let's not try to fly before we can flap, as Mother used to say. We've got the beginnings of an idea, a good idea, a revolutionary idea. That is to use the girls as the spearhead (for I'm sure that everyone else will have a part to play when the plan's complete) of an attack upon the long-noses. All we know so far is that one of them chanced to lay an egg in flight and that egg chanced to hit a long-nose. So now we've got to wait until, first, they're all in full lay and, second, they all prove to be able to lay in flight; and when that's happened, we must arrange for them to have masses of practice and to get into really good training. By that time, by the grace of Chanticleer, someone may have had a brain wave about the problem of hardening the eggs."

At that there was a murmur of agreement, and the family flew off about their day's business.

Within a few days, Ransome, Sims, and Jefferies were able to report that they had all laid, and by the end of a week they were laying daily. At first they had difficulty in controlling the timing of egg laying, and would drop one when and where the urge came upon them, to begin with even on the bare earth of the farmyard. Farmer Farmer was always grateful for this early random laying of pullets, for it saved him the usual laborious climb up his tallest ladder to the high nesting places. But gradually they became more expert in discharging an egg at a time of their own choosing, and one morning they came to their parents to say that they had not yet laid that day's eggs and were ready to attempt a lay in flight.

Spillers and Massey-Harris had already decided on the duck pond as a practice bombing range, for a number of reasons. First, it was untenanted, for the foxes had long since exterminated the ducks; second, it was the right distance—a hundred yards —from a suitable takeoff spot—the roof of the Dutch barn, which provided both height for a diving attack and a fine vantage point for observing accuracy of aim; third—and the adult birds considered this important—its use meant that the practice eggs would sink out of sight and reach, so that neither would the sisters be upset nor vermin encouraged by the sight of smashed eggs splattered all over the place, as would have happened on a solid target; and fourth, common sense told them it was hardly likely to contain large numbers of submerged foxes. Lastly, by a happy chance, an old discarded tire from a tractor had at some time floated out to a point three quarters of the way down the length of the pond, and had there become anchored in a small cluster of rushes, providing the perfect bull's-eye.

The three sisters had chosen their time carefully. They had made certain that their nine brothers were out foraging, and had picked a moment when their mother and father were together on the Dutch barn roof.

"All right," said Massey-Harris. "Who's going first?"

"I don't think I can hold it much longer," giggled Jefferies agitatedly, and launching herself off, she slid down the curve of the roof on her front, gently picking up speed until, at the edge, she spread wide her powerful wings and began to glide toward the duck pond. Her direction was perfect but her airspeed slow, and for one reason or another, she released her cargo too early. "Egg gone!" they heard her gasp, and as she flattened out and skimmed the surface of the water, they saw the egg, turning end over end in the air, splash into the near part of the pond.

As the parents cried, "Short!" Sims began to slide down the roof but, profiting from what she had seen, gave half a dozen strong wing beats as soon as she was clear of the edge before settling into the glide. She released her egg from a slightly higher altitude than had her sister and passed perhaps six feet above the pond's surface; but still the telltale splash was no more than a third of the way down the long rectangle of green scummy water.

"Can you hang on a minute, dear?" said Spillers to Ransome.

"Yes, I'm okay, Mom," said Ransome. "I think I know what you're going to say. The others weren't going fast enough, were they? I mean their eggs were not only dropping short; they were falling too slowly. I could see them turning over and over, when to my mind they ought to be going like lightning."

"Exactly," said Spillers. "Don't glide at all, Ransome darling. When you get off the edge of the roof, point yourself at the target and fly like blazes. And don't release till the last possible moment."

"Right," said Ransome, "here we go," and she proceeded to follow her mother's instructions to the letter.

As she pulled up into a steep climb at the far end after a run down the pond at wood-pigeon speed, the observers saw her egg drill into the water not six feet from the target.

"Oh, that's more like it!" shouted Massey-Harris. "Couldn't have done better my—er, that is to say, couldn't have been done better, could it, my dear?"

"Yes, it could," replied Spillers shortly. "It could

have been a direct hit. Direct hits are what we need. And we'll get them soon, you'll see."

The near miss had been close enough, however, for the resulting splash to wet the old tire and to throw up into relief the lettering on its muddy wall. As Ransome, after a controlled stall at the top of her climb, dived down and glided back over the target, she read on it the name GOODYEAR.

"Gosh!" she thought, "Great-Granny's name. Perhaps that's a lucky sign. She was a pretty hard-boiled old bird."

10
The Brain Wave

POULTRY, OF COURSE, HAVE SHORT MEMORIES, often completely forgetting what has happened a few hours earlier, and cannot possibly use, as we do, such a term as *anniversary*. Even for the highly intelligent Foxearth flock, though individual birds occasionally recalled incidents that had happened a long time ago, the span of a year was too much to remember. Sometimes, however, when some remarkable event had occurred, they remembered its *monaversary*, a term derived from an old Hennish word *mona*, meaning a lunar month.

Thus it was that Ransome, Sims, and Jefferies, their morning's practice runs completed, were thinking gravely of the great raid, twenty-eight days after that dreadful slaughter. They were perched side by side in the top branches of a tall dead elm, from which vantage point they could look down into the walled garden and see the fruit pen, its door wide open still, for there was no fruit to protect.

It was now late July, and ever since the raid a heat wave had persisted, with endless days of blazing sunshine and very high temperatures; even the nights were uncomfortably hot. There had been no sign of the long-noses, and the "masses of practice" and "really good training" which Spillers had insisted upon had resulted in the three pullets reaching an astonishing degree of accuracy in their bombing.

On most days each of them had an egg ready, so that two and sometimes three attacks would be flown each morning. And two and sometimes three times each morning a splash would arise from the very center of the target ring formed by the old tractor tire, as an egg whistled into the water, launched at maximum speed.

Any hen that lays an egg greets the event with wild yells of excitement and shouts of joy and surprise, and the three were no exception as each climbed and soared away from the duck pond, the loud crows of their father on the Dutch barn roof signaling yet another bull's-eye. They were now completely confident in their own abilities, and in no way worried that the duck pond, due to the continuing drought, was fast drying up and would soon be of no further use as a range. They could hit a long-nose, of that they were sure—hit him right slap bang between the eyes; but what was the use of that if the missile simply provided the fox with a bit of a shock and a free meal to lick off his ugly face?

It was Ransome who spoke first. "Do you know what I'd like to do this monaversary?" she said slowly.

"What?" said the other two.

"I'd like," she said, "to get hold of those four long-noses and shut 'em in that greenhouse. I bet it's like an ov—whoops, I mean, like a furnace in there."

Indeed, since the raid Farmer Farmer had been so dispirited that he seemed to have lost interest in his garden; all the windows of the greenhouse were tight shut and even its sliding door was only open six inches.

"I'd like to sit around," Ransome went on, "and watch them pant and sweat in there until they were"—and she hesitated—"well, I don't care if it is fowl language, until they were *boiled*."

Her sisters raised their combs slightly, and then Jefferies said with a giggle, "Yes, I suppose anything that stayed in there for any length of time would be . . . what you said."

"We would, if we went in there," said Sims seriously. She nodded her head a good many times to give weight to this opinion, while Jefferies continued to chuckle. Both these activities were abruptly cut short by Ransome's next words. As always she was the leader, in thought as well as action, and now she was thinking ahead of her sisters.

"If it was hot enough," she said, "perhaps even the eggs inside us would become . . ." She paused and looked at her sisters, whose beaks, already slightly open from the heat of the day, now fell wide as they grasped her meaning.

Excitedly they began to discuss the brain wave.

"Hard enough to give a long-nose something to think about?"

"Perhaps hard enough to stop him ever thinking again."

"I suppose it must be terribly hot in there."

"Must be. Except for the very early morning, it's in the full glare of the sun all day."

"And what a sun. The elders say there's never been such heat."

"And the wall's quite near it. That must reflect even more heat onto it."

"And it's almost completely sealed. Just a crack at the door."

They paused for breath.

"Nothing could live in it—plants, I mean," said Jefferies.

"Something could die in it," said Sims slowly.

"Yes," said Ransome very deliberately. "We could. We certainly should, I imagine, if we rushed things. We must do it gradually. It may not work—as far as the eggs are concerned. We can only find that out by trying. And it will expose us to the risk —of death."

"And we can only find that out by frying," said Jefferies with a shout of laughter.

Five minutes later one was perched above the gate of the walled garden—for the height of the walls meant of course that this was the only way by which a prowling long-nose could disturb them —while the other two, keyed up to instant readiness for flight, nervously approached the greenhouse. They could see that the structure itself held nothing but the skeletons of dead tomato plants, but they remembered vividly the ambush place under the table at the rear. Suddenly, from either side, they smashed into the flanking piles of clay flower pots, beating at them with their strong wings, their brave hearts thudding at the fear of what might lie within. But as the pots shattered and the sunlight streamed in, the space below the table was seen to be quite empty, and only a few long red hairs showed the use to which it had been put.

One pullet now slipped inside the greenhouse and, jumping up onto the slatted wooden scaffolding which ran along one side, sat motionless for a few minutes. Then she gave place to the sister waiting outside and flew up to relieve the gate guard; so that after eight or nine minutes all three sisters had made trial of the heat within. It was already so great that the mercury in the little wooden-cased thermometer was jammed against the top of the tube, indicating some fearful temperature far in excess of the maximum reading of one hundred and twenty degrees. Then nervously, excitedly, thirstily, they flew out of the walled garden in their customary tight formation, to find the family.

11
The Climbers

DURING ALL THIS TIME, THE FOUR SUCCESSFUL RAID-
ers, the memory of the great slaughter and feast
constantly in their thoughts and dreams, had been
by no means idle. The most intelligent of their
kind, as were the three pullets of theirs, they revolved a number of plans in their minds before
deciding upon an idea and proceeding to train for
it. Although they had carefully kept away from the
farmhouse and buildings since the great raid, they
had come fairly close during their hunting after
less tasty prey; and in particular had visited an old
and rather tumbledown shed which stood in the
middle of a field half a mile away. In this shed was
a stack of straw bales, against which leaned a short
ladder of no more than eight or nine rungs. And
among the bales lived a colony of rats, fat from a
diet of grain stolen from a patch of barley ripening
nearby.

Most of the foxes' hunting of these rats was done
at night, when they jumped the barley eaters in
their runs between shed and field; but one day they
came in daylight, and as they slipped into the
building the rats, not surprisingly, were nowhere

to be seen, having taken refuge on the very top of the straw stack. They could be heard, squeaking and chattering with excitement, but their talk was all in Rodent, a language common to all such creatures as mice, voles, shrews, rabbits, and squirrels, but quite unintelligible to the foxes, who spoke and understood nothing but Vulpine.

They now chatted among themselves in this tongue as they lay on the earth floor of the old shed and listened to the rats.

"That ladder," said one, "reminds me. There's a ladder leaning up against the hay in the Dutch barn at the farm."

The ladder in fact was usually there. It provided the means for Farmer Farmer to collect his breakfast eggs.

"So what?" said another. "Foxes can't climb ladders."

"Foxes haven't climbed ladders. Yet," said the third.

There was a pause.

"You mean . . . ?" said the fourth.

They looked at each other.

"That ladder at the farm," said the first speaker. "It's a very long one." It was in fact a thirty-two runger. "Very long."

"But if we learned . . ." said the second.

". . . to climb this one . . ." said the third.

There was a pause.

"You mean . . . ?" said the fourth, and with that perfect timing and mutual understanding that made them such a great team, three of the foxes ranged themselves in a line below the stack, poised, ready, staring up at it, while the fourth, one of the brothers, threw himself at the short ladder and began to climb. His ascent was by no means expert; twice his feet slipped between the rungs and his brush whirled wildly around and around in his efforts to balance himself; but he succeeded, and vanished from the others' sight into the gloomy space between the top of the stack and the roof of the shed.

They heard a wild chorus of squeals as he pounced and chopped among the barley eaters, and then one, two, three cartwheeling gray shapes came flying over the edge as he flicked them to the catchers below before, half leaping, half sliding, he

63

dropped down to join them with a fourth gray body clamped in his long jaws.

So a scheme was born, a scheme which would call for determination, agility, and courage. The foxes had all these things.

Thus, while one side was hard at work on the practice bombing range in the duck pond, the other perfected its climbing technique on the short ladder in the old shed. Partly to compensate for its lack of length, and partly because they realized that, having made the ascent of the Dutch barn and done their dirty work among such fowls as they would find on top of the hay, they would still have to get down to the ground again, the foxes practiced not only going up but also coming down—backward, because they didn't fancy pointing their long noses down the almost vertical slope of the thirty-two runger. Soon they became expert, placing their neat feet exactly upon the rungs in exactly the right order, so that they seemed to flow up onto the the top of the straw from which the surviving rats had long since emigrated in terror at this continual invasion.

The foxes knew that descending would be a much slower matter, but they decided that they were prepared to take the risk, for by then, with luck, they would have spilled a good deal of blood. They knew that when they reached the summit, any poultry there could easily escape them by flight, but they suspected (rightly) that the top surface of the stack of hay bales was a favorite hatching and brooding area; they planned to kill mother birds on the nest, both those who might sit tight on unhatched eggs and those who might try to protect their tiny chicks; and the chicks themselves, they thought greedily, would make delicious little mouthfuls.

Above all, they knew that, as in the case of the great raid, the one thing essential to their success was surprise. They must be up that long ladder like four spiders running up a wall. They had no special respect for farmer and dogs, though they knew they must not dally. At least the hens couldn't hurt them, they sniggered to one another.

12
The Greenhouse

MASSEY-HARRIS, SPILLERS, AND THE NINE YOUNG cockerels listened in silence as the three sisters told them what they had done on that hot monaversary morning. When their report was finished and while they were still panting with excitement and from the heat of their trial moments under glass, it was Massey-Harris who spoke first.

"I think it's madness," he squawked angrily. "Fancy going voluntarily into that deathtrap of a garden again."

"That's where the only greenhouse is, Father," said Sims.

"Yes, and that's another thing," her father said. "Even supposing this addlepated plan should work —as far as the eggs are concerned, I mean—that sort of heat will kill you before you ever get to fly at another long-nose."

"Not if we acclimatize to it," said Jefferies.

"Gradually," said Ransome.

As usual, it was Spillers who quickly thought the whole thing out and summed up her reactions. "If it's going to be tried, it'll have to be quick," she said, "in case the weather breaks and before those

66

murderers reappear. As regards them, you girls will have to be well protected while you're in the hot spot, so we'll all stand guard. You'll certainly have to come to it gradually, or you'll prove your father right; say, five minutes the first day, and then add five a day—that's, let's see, half an hour in six days' time; keep that half hour up every day for another week and that should be long enough, but you simply won't know till you fly your first attack after you've been under glass for that time. That greenhouse ought to heat up pretty early in this weather, so you shouldn't have to hold back your times of lay all that long" *(provided,* she thought to herself, *those* omelettes *of long-noses come at the right time).* "In fact," Spillers finished, "all you girls have got to decide is whether you're going to do your heat training all together, or whether one of you's going to go it alone in case, er, something goes wrong."

"All together, Mom," said Ransome, Sims, and Jefferies with one voice.

"Well, I must say, M-H," said Spillers, turning to her husband and speaking with a lump in her crop, "thank Chanticleer for a good drop of game-bird blood."

So the very next morning, by five to nine, when the thermometer in the almost closed greenhouse already registered one hundred and twenty degrees in that exceptional heat wave, the scene was set in the old walled garden of Foxearth Farm. Massey-Harris, who could tell the time, having been hatched out on a high ledge just under the stable clock, was to be timekeeper. From the top of the tall dead elm, he could just see the face of that same clock over the roof of the milking parlor. The boldest of the nine brothers (he who had asked about hard-boiled eggs—his name was Icky) perched above the open garden gate and of his eight brothers, two sat upon each of the four walls, facing outward. Spillers positioned herself imme-diately outside the greenhouse door, so as to be ready to rush in and drag out any of the pullets who might become prostrated by the heat. Every eye was cocked. The distant clock began to strike the hour and the big rooster's crow confirmed it. Before his voice had died away, the three sisters were sitting motionless upon the greenhouse scaf-folding for their first five-minute spell.

As soon as another cry from the rooster told that time was up, the three came out of the greenhouse and all fourteen birds took off and flew thankfully away from the hated place. They glided into the cool of the barn and settled together on Massey-Harris's night perch, high in the dimness of the roof space. The pullets, still panting a little, were questioned by the rest of the family. "Are you all right?" "Will you be able to stand it for longer?" "What was it like?" To all of which they replied that they were, that they would, and that it was *very* hot —the last a bit crossly, as happens when stupid questions are asked. Then, only half heeding Spillers's cry of "Think before you drink!" they slipped down to a cattle trough to quench their thirst.

On the fourth day of the heat trials they had just begun the twenty-minute stretch, when Massey-Harris from the elm and all the guards from the wall simultaneously gave the alarm.

"Out! Sharp!" called Spillers, and all four females quickly took off and climbed steeply to join the males who were gaining height to find out the cause of the trouble which had filled the sky over the house and buildings with flying fowls, shouting and squawking their agitation.

Suddenly they saw, at the far end of the yard, four long-noses slip out under the gate and trot calmly and quietly away toward the woods.

"Dad! Mom!" cried Ransome, Sims, and Jefferies. "Shall we have a go?"

"Yes, have a bash!" yelled the nine cockerels, while the big rooster's neck feathers rose in a great

ruff, his comb and wattles grew purple with rage, and he looked as though he would take on the hated enemy single clawed.

"Let's show 'em we're not chicken!" he bawled, as the family circled a hundred feet above the foxes. But Spillers's voice rang out, cutting the cackle and bringing them all to their senses.

"Wait!" she cried, "it's too early. Wait till the heat training's finished. You'd only make a mess of it now. When we hit them, we've got to hit them hard." *I was afraid those* scrambled *long-noses would come before we were ready,* she swore to herself. *Yet they didn't stay long and they don't seem to have done any damage. I wonder what happened?*

13
The Strange Business

WHAT HAD HAPPENED WAS THIS. THE FOUR LONG-
noses had chosen that day to mount their ladder
attack. They were trained to a red hair, their plans
were made, and they knew that if they delayed
much longer at this time of the year there would be
fewer nests on top of the hay bales. They had decided the order in which they would tackle the ascent and had come in Indian file to a point on a
little hump of ground from which they could see
the milking parlor. They knew that at a certain
time—it was around nine o'clock—the farmer, his
milking and dairy work completed, would leave
the parlor and walk through the barnyard into the
farmhouse for his breakfast. As with the great raid,
they calculated that they needed about three minutes of uninterrupted time for their business. Flat
upon the ground, the leader peered through a big
plant of yellow ragwort, and saw Farmer Farmer
come out of the parlor and walk away followed by
his dogs who had been lying outside. The foxes
waited.

As the farmer walked past the Dutch barn, he
remembered something. The previous day, as he

came out of his back door, he had seen one of his hens fly from a certain spot, shouting with triumph. This spot was where the roof of the farmhouse met the roof of an old cart shed which he used as a garage; the two roofs meeting formed a V where, in dry weather, he had found nests in the past. He thought he would investigate this place for his breakfast eggs.

With practiced ease, he picked up the thirty-two runger from its place against the hay bales and, holding it vertically, carried it away to the house. He placed it against the wall, climbed about halfway up it, took off his cap, and reached round the side of the ladder. The nest was exactly where he had thought, and leaving one egg in it, he put the other three in his cap, climbed one handed down again, and walked into his house.

A few moments later, the four foxes moved. Each had acquired mental maps during their early unsuccessful hunting, and they had planned their route from the little hillock carefully.

First they ran, nose to tail, down the blind side of a hedge until they reached a point not twenty yards from the farmyard; here the hedge gave out, but a ditch continued (bone dry in the drought) and along this they crept until they reached the boundary, which at this point was a short stretch of wall. There was a drain hole in the bottom of the wall, through which the leader poked a cautious head and, seeing no sign of any watchful chicken, led

the others swiftly along a narrow passage between the walls of two adjacent buildings.

The planners had reckoned first, that no bird was likely to venture into so cramped and dangerous a space—for above all things they were anxious to avoid a premature alarm—and second, that this passage would bring them to a point as near as they could possibly get to the foot of the long ladder.

Lying now in their single file at the head of the passage, each knew that in turn he or she must swing sharp right at the moment of emerging into the open, and that then all that remained was a lightning dash of ten or fifteen yards to the foot of the ladder. They could see nothing from where they lay, but in their minds was the exact position of the long wooden contraption that was to be their pathway to another glorious blood-soaked slaughter! They tensed every muscle.

When the foxes shot out, skidding around the corner to aim themselves at the Dutch barn, the yard was full of foraging fowls. On the instant all were airborne, and the air was filled with wildly beating birds and many loud cries of "Long-long-long-nose! Long-long-long-nose!" which alerted the family down at the walled garden.

On top of the great stack of hay bales many mothers sat smugly brooding, confident of their safe position and ignorant of danger.

What occurred next was a tribute to the intelligence of the four raiders; not for nothing had they already achieved more than their elders had done in a lifetime. As soon as they focused on the side of the barn, they saw of course that the thirty-two runger was gone. Immediately each knew that the mission was impossible, that they must call it off, but above all that they must give the cloud of circling screaming chickens no clue as to what they had been going to do or where they had been aiming to attack.

In a flash they all turned sharp at right angles again and galloped across the yard in line, four abreast, as though to attack the area of the milking parlor. They turned again, back into file, and charged the farrowing house. Then, one last ninety-degree turn bringing them into line once more, they ran shoulder to shoulder through the great barn, out through its farthest doors, cantered to the gate at the far end of the yard, slipped under, and trotted calmly and quietly away toward the woods.

When Farmer Farmer came running from his bacon-and-eggs to find out the cause of the hullabaloo, he was as puzzled as his fowls over the object of the raid.

Later that day, the family were discussing the whole strange business with other birds who had been in the yard at the time.

"Can't figure it out at all," said an old International Harvester, scratching his graying head with his right foot. "What in the name of Chanticleer did those long-noses think they were doing?"

"It seemed like a sort of dance," said three hens called Sainsbury, Silcocks, and Simplex all together. "First running this way, then that. No sense in it."

"Could they have been rehearsing for something?" said a Trespassers.

"Well, that's an idea," said Massey-Harris, "but I can't see what they could hope to achieve in broad daylight when all the nonfliers"—by which he meant of course young chicks and their mothers—"are perfectly safe up in the high places like the top of the Dutch barn."

"At any rate they did no damage," said Spillers.

"Let's hope today's performance, whatever it was in aid of, may mean they won't come again for a bit." *Time,* she thought to herself, *we must have more time. Another ten days, in fact.*

14
The Trials

NEXT DAY THE FAMILY BEGAN THE HEAT TRAINING at the point where they had been rudely interrupted, that is to say, the twenty-minute stretch. When this was successfully completed, the three sisters went away to their various chosen places to lay their daily eggs.

Now it happened that Ransome was using a blocked-up snow box—a square black funnel beside the roof designed to pass the rainwater, from the horizontal gutters into the down pipe. This pipe fed into a great water barrel in the yard, thirty feet below. The top of the water barrel was covered with wooden slats, except for one little gap where the down pipe entered it; and on this sun-warmed platform one of the many farm cats lay curled fast asleep in the heat of the morning.

Peering over the edge of the snow box as she settled herself before laying, Ransome found herself looking straight down on to the broad tabby back far below, and she was suddenly filled with an impulse of pure mischief such as is often felt by young creatures. Without really considering what she was doing, and certainly not in any spirit of scientific investigation, she turned herself around on the nest so that she was facing the wall of the building, and raising herself slightly so that her bottom stuck out over the rim of the snow box, she laid. Her customary yells of pleasure were suddenly cut short as, swiveling around to look downward—half expecting perhaps to see a surprised tomcat rudely awakened by the explosion somewhere near him of an egg dropped from thirty feet —she saw instead his broad tabby stomach as he lay on the ground beside the butt. The egg had in fact struck him squarely on the top of his big round head and, bouncing off, now lay on the floor beside him—cracked but not smashed! The tom had been knocked out cold. All four legs stuck up in the air and on his unconscious face was a stupid grin.

After a couple of minutes he opened his eyes, shook his head, staggered to his feet, and weaved and wobbled drunkenly away across the yard. The heat training was beginning to work!

There was tremendous excitement when a wildly gabbling Ransome told her story to the rest; and all three pullets begged to be allowed to fly trial sorties against the very next fox that showed his long nose around the farm. But Spillers, delighted though she was at this indication that the treatment was beginning to succeed and anxious as she was to mount a counterattack against the next invasion, strove to calm them down.

"We must be more certain," she said. "Let's be

patient until we've finished the program, and then the very next day after that you can fly some proper trials, I promise. Your time'll come, sure as eggs is eggs."

At last the program was completed. While the weather seemed to grow hotter and hotter, Ransome, Sims, and Jefferies had sweated out the shaping-up part of the heat training and had successfully occupied the sweltering greenhouse for thirty minutes a day for a further week. The time had come for the trials.

Spillers and Massey-Harris had given a good deal of thought to these. They had decided, very reasonably, that Farmer Farmer would not be par-

ticularly pleased at the sight of numbers of cats and perhaps dogs lying about the place unconscious or worse. Also they were not concerned with selecting targets simply for their small size; they were confident of the pullets' skill in precision bombing. What they needed to do was to select some object or material which would give a good idea of the strike power of the egg missiles.

At last they fixed upon a black polyethylene rick sheet which covered a large and somewhat collapsed heap of last year's straw bales at the far end of the farmyard. Because of the heap's domelike shape, the sheet covered it rather like a tent; it thus presented plenty of good sloping surfaces to aim at, and hits would be easy to record if, as they hoped, the eggs penetrated the material.

They realized, of course, that even heavy-duty polyethylene is a lot less tough than the skull of a long-nose, but they thought it a reasonable idea in the circumstances, considering the time factor involved. The foxes, they thought, might be back at any minute. In this they were wrong. The raiders, from a distant daylight vantage point, could see that the thirty-two runger still stood against the farmhouse wall.

The trials themselves were moderately successful. Only a maximum of three missiles a day could be discharged, of course, but on the first day Ransome, Sims, and Jefferies all obliged simultaneously, and when their joint shout of "Egg gone!" rang out as they wheeled away beyond the straw heap, the family could see three holes in the blackness of the rick sheet.

The eggs were strong enough to pierce the sheet, but their shells were still badly cracked by the impact. The eggs were only softboiled. So each day for yet another week the pullets subjected themselves to longer and yet longer spells in the furnacelike greenhouse (Ransome actually achieving forty minutes), and each day the trials went on, until the rick sheet began to look like a colander. And still the foxes did not come.

15
The Hard Way

AS THE TENSION MOUNTED, SO TEMPERS BECAME A little frayed. The eggs still were not hard enough to be lethal, and it was becoming obvious to the family that some reinforcement was needed to supplement the training in the greenhouse. Strangely, a simpler possible method of egg hardening had been overlooked. It took a little family squabble to provide the stimulus for the right line of thought.

It happened on the last day of that week's trials. On recovery for examination the last three eggs still had cracked shells, though their contents were firm enough. There was a general feeling of frustration; things were so nearly right, but in the face of such imminent danger "nearly" was not good enough. Icky, who like his father was often tactless to a degree, triggered it off: "Looks like you three will have to sit in that old greenhouse all day long," he said with something between a snigger and a chuckle. "These old eggs wouldn't knock out a rat."

This was too much for the sisters, and fowl language began to fly.

"You stupid scrambled boy!" shouted Sims.

"Go and fricassee yourself!" yelled Ransome.

"Just like a cockerel!" screamed Jefferies. "Nothing to do all day long but sit about and crow, while a pullet's work is never done. Lucky you weren't hatched a female. You'd have been a layabout, for sure. Probably you'd have been a softshell!"

Of these last two Hennish insults, a "layabout" was a bird so casual and feckless in its laying habits that it would drop eggs anywhere and everywhere without any concern for the rules of nest work, while "softshell" referred derisively to a bird so stupid or unnatural as not to eat sufficient quantities of grit to provide its eggs with a proper shell covering; such birds therefore on occasion laid horrid wobbly things of no possible use for hatching and only fit for the farmer to pick up gingerly and break into a cup for some unthinkable use of his own. By no stretch of the imagination was either term applicable to Icky, but in their anger the other two pullets took up Jefferies's last word, and all three shouted at their brother, "Softshell! Softshell! Softshell!"

Icky turned very red, while his eight brothers looked down their beaks in embarrassment. Spillers seemed about to speak, but before she could open her beak Massey-Harris voiced his extreme disapproval of the proceedings.

"Stop!" he cried. "Stop this disgraceful bickering immediately. I really don't know what things are coming to when young girls like you squawk in such a fashion. In my young day pullets were seen and not heard. Leave the yard at once. And as for you, sir," he went on, rounding upon Icky, "I'm surprised you can't find better things to do than spending your time teasing your sisters. Be off with you, and take your brothers with you, unless you want to feel the weight of my wing."

Left alone with his wife, he settled his ruffled feathers, snapped his beak self-importantly a couple of times, and glanced sideways at Spillers to see her reaction to this fine display of fatherly authority. Spillers remained silent, looking thoughtful. Massey-Harris was a little disappointed at her lack of response; he was also beginning to feel slightly ashamed of his outburst, for he was at heart devoted to his children in the soppiest way, especially to his daughters.

"I cannot think what's got into—" he started to say, when his wife interrupted him.

"Look, M-H," she said, "help me to think something through a minute."

Spillers had in fact thought the something through already, in her usual incisive way, but she knew that an appeal to her husband would please and settle him.

"Let's play a little game," she went on. "I'll ask you some questions and you give me the answers. What do chickens need beside grain and meal and pellets and water?"

"Ah!" said Massey-Harris. "Now—let's see. Green vegetables are most acceptable; spring cabbage— broccoli—lettuce, yes, especially lettuce."

"No," said Spillers, "I didn't mean that."

"Well, fruit is very delicious," said Massey-Harris, "like . . ." he paused awkwardly, suddenly realizing with horror where this suggestion was leading. *Oh, my comb and wattles!* he thought, *I nearly said "strawberries."*

"No," said Spillers coldly, "no."

"Oh, worms!" cried the rooster hastily. "Lovely fat red wriggling worms. They go down like candy."

"No, no, no," said his wife.

"I know—wood lice!" said Massey-Harris, his comb rising in excitement. "I personally enjoy wood lice very much. They're so crunchy."

"No, no, no, no!" Spillers said impatiently. "I didn't ask what chickens like. I asked what they need."

"Oh, sorry, old girl," said her husband hastily. "I

85

see what you're getting at now. They need grit." He was a little crestfallen.

"And why do chickens need grit?" she continued.

"Well, let me see now," said Massey-Harris, beginning to enjoy the little game, as it seemed now to be giving him the chance to hold forth in his fine voice upon a subject which he knew all about, the chance in fact to give a lecture. "Chickens need grit for two reasons; and, what's more, they need grit of two types. You see, you have to understand that there is soluble grit and insoluble grit, that is to say a kind that will dissolve and a kind that won't dissolve."

He looked sideways at Spillers to see how she was taking all this, but she made no comment; indeed, she appeared to be marking his discourse with care and attention.

"They need soluble grit," he went on, "like limestone grit or oystershell, to provide them with calcium for making good bone in their bodies and good shell on their eggs. And they need insoluble grit, like flint or gravel or any little bits of stony stuff, to help them to grind up their food efficiently."

He stopped.

"Anything else you'd like to know?" he said.

"This limestone and oystershell," said Spillers. "You say it makes good shell on eggs. What happens if hens don't get it or don't get enough of it?"

"Well," replied Massey-Harris, scratching the back of his neck ruff very rapidly with his right foot to mask his confusion, "that's what makes your, um—er, that's what makes your 'softshell,'" he concluded in a low voice.

"So too little of this soluble grit gives eggs soft shells?" said Spillers.

"Yes. You know that quite well."

"What does the right amount of grit give them?"

"Why, the right sort of shells, of course."

"What do you call the right sort of shells?"

"Oh, really, my dear . . . why, not too soft and not too hard."

"So what would a tremendous enormous whacking great lot of grit give them?" said Spillers quietly.

"Well, obviously," said Massey-Harris impatiently, "it would give them very hard . . ." he paused, and then excitedly, "terribly hard . . ."—he gulped—"murderously hard shells!" he shouted at the top of his voice. "Of course, of course, of course! Why didn't I think of it before? We must put the girls onto double, treble, quadruple rations of limestone and oystershell straight away. Carry on with the heat training, of course, at the same time as we pack 'em full of as much grit as their crops will carry! Yes, of course! By Chanticleer, I'm glad I was able to think that one through for you, old lady."

"I'm glad you were, M-H," said Spillers gently.

So it was arranged. Farmer Farmer supplied limestone and oystershell grit for his hens, putting out a supply in three or four old wooden boxes at various places. The family agreed, however, that this would not possibly be enough to provide Ransome, Sims, and Jefferies with vast extra quantities without depriving all the other laying birds of the flock. So Massey-Harris slipped into the shed where the poultry food was kept—the corn and meal and pellets in huge ratproof bins, but the grit in paper bags—and with his strong beak tore open one of the bags at the back, nearest the wall, where the break would not be noticed.

And every day, as well as continuing their daily half hour in the greenhouse, the gallant trio now crammed themselves as full as they could with the clean sharp silvery grit. When humans say that someone is "full of grit," they mean full of courage. Before long the sisters were to prove that they were filled with grit in both senses of the word.

16
The Ringleader

Ransome, even more than her sisters, combined the finest qualities of her parents. Moreover, she had inherited Spillers's shrewdness without that overlay of excessive caution with which her mother addressed every problem, and Massey-Harris's courage without the hotheadedness which was his trademark. More importantly, she was not simply better equipped than Sims and Jefferies. She knew she was. And most importantly, she was not conceited about this knowledge. Increasingly, as the family and the rest of the flock waited for what all felt would be a fight to a finish, Ransome thought hard about the part she had to play, a part which she felt strongly would be vital. She could not, of course, know exactly what was in store for her, but she knew, somehow, that she was destined for some final all-important struggle with the enemy.

So at roost time, when all the head scratching and preening and feather settling was done, she perched and thought, long after the rest were sound asleep. Despite her proven skills, something had been worrying her for a long time now. Of her

physical abilities she was not in any doubt. Just as the Foxearthers were vastly more skilled than ordinary fowls, and she and her sisters far superior to the rest of the flock, so she knew that in strength, speed, maneuverability, and accuracy she was the best. What worried her was the realization that, despite all her great gifts, she, like chickens everywhere, could not overcome the one great built-in fear; she was still, at heart, very frightened of foxes. And gradually, unavoidably, because she could not only outact but also outthink the rest, she came to a conclusion. Like all truly brave individuals, she realized that the only way to fight fear is to look it in the face. She must go to the woods, find the foxes, confront them on their own ground. Only thus, she felt sure, could she build in herself that supreme confidence for the final act.

One morning, then, her mind made up, she set

off. She had done her greenhouse spell, eaten her extra grit, and, particularly, laid that day's egg in flight on the rick-sheet range so as to go unarmed, trusting only in her powers of flight and her wits. She had said nothing of her plan to the rest, and made sure her departure was not noted. For lack of any better direction, she flew along the line of retreat which the four foxes had taken on that strange day when they had run about the farmyard in so odd a fashion. After flying for two or three miles, she suddenly saw below her exactly the kind of place for which she had been looking. It was a grassy clearing, as big as a football field, in the middle of the woods; and in the center of the clearing stood a solitary beech tree; she glided toward it and pitched in the upper branches. Looking down, she saw that one great branch stuck out, parallel with the ground and about eight feet above it—just above fox jump, in fact; she dropped onto it, settled her feathers, and waited.

For a long time, nothing happened. Constantly swiveling her head, Ransome watched the circle of trees surrounding the clearing. Because, like all birds, she had no sense of smell, she had to rely on her eyes, and could not tell from the sharp stink, as a squirrel could have done, that there was already a fox hiding behind the beech's great trunk. He had run in a straight line from the wood, keeping the trunk between himself and the pullet. But before he could decide what next to do, the fringe of the clearing on the downwind side was suddenly alive

with four, five, six pointed faces of long-noses drawn irresistibly by the breeze's message. And before long a dozen or more adult foxes and some part-grown cubs sat in a rough circle below Ransome's branch, and stared, and passed their tongues ceaselessly over their long white fangs.

This was the moment when any ordinary fowl would have panicked into a fluttering attempt at escape, or simply toppled, mesmerized, down into the jaws below. This was the moment, also, that Ransome was waiting for, had planned for, had thought about endlessly. Now she must look them in the eyes, each and every one of them, squarely and unflinchingly. And she did, sitting quite motionless except for the regular movement of her downbent head as one after another the foxes met her hard, cold, unblinking gaze, and one after another they dropped their eyes before the stare, some growling, some snarling a little, some whining in a kind of embarrassment.

Suddenly a big dog fox, he who had hid behind the tree, ran and launched himself in a great leap at the pullet; but his teeth clacked together a yard below her claws, and all he got for his pains was a particularly icy and penetrating look followed by a huge yawn as Ransome opened her gape to its widest in a gesture of utter contempt.

At this the foxes' control broke, and one after another they ran and leapt and missed and leapt again, snarling and barking and even snapping at one another. One or two tried to climb the trunk of the tree, but the beech's smooth silvery skin did not give them enough hold to reach the crotch of the branch on which the maddening bird sat.

Newcomers came out of the woods, attracted by the rumpus, and eventually there were a couple of dozen long-nosed chicken-lovers sitting, lying, or pacing restlessly beneath the branch. They began to talk among themselves, and though Ransome could not understand a word, Vulpine being a totally different language from Hennish, she listened to the horrid yowly voices and, while she listened, planned her final move.

"Mum," said the biggest of the cubs to its mother, "it'll have to come down sooner or later, won't it? When it gets hungry or thirsty enough, I mean?"

"Silly child," was the reply. "That's a Foxearth

fowl. They can fly. When it's ready, it'll just fly away."

"It doesn't make any noise, does it?" said another cub.

"Oh, they can't talk, like us. All the foolish things can do is squawk."

"Funny, though," said one of the other adult foxes, "this one somehow doesn't seem to be frightened of us. That's what annoys me about the stupid thing. Still, I suppose it's worth waiting. There may be something wrong with it. I mean, what on earth is it doing right out here, miles from the farm?"

Among the waiting pack were the four young raiders. Of all the foxes there, they, with the memory of their feast still fresh in their minds, were perhaps the most coldly furious at the sheer impudence of this solitary intruder into their country. One of them—one of the two vixens—walked forward until she stood directly beneath Ransome. Then she reared up on her hind legs, and in a thin snarling voice shaking with anger, she said, "I have a strange feeling that we shall meet again one day, you and I."

Ransome blinked owlishly, and the vixen dropped back on all fours with a low growl.

Ransome had now been sitting on the branch of the beech tree for nearly an hour, and thought it time to make for home. On the one hand she had proved to her own satisfaction that she was battle ready, that she could stand the fire of those terrible green eyes without flinching. On the other hand she saw no point in prolonging the confrontation, for by now her absence from home would have been noticed and she did not want to worry the family; it was easy to imagine her father in his anxiety sending search patrols all over the place and thus weakening the defenses. However, she did not wish to end the affair by simply taking the easy way out and flying effortlessly away from her enemies. While they had been talking, she had been thinking, and now at last the kind of opportunity for which she had been hoping presented itself.

The adult foxes had all stayed close by the tree, waiting, watchful for any possible chance which might reward their patience; but the cubs, like youngsters everywhere, became bored by inactivity and began a series of rough-and-tumble games out in the grass of the clearing. The biggest of the cubs, however, was all by itself, for it had discovered an interesting hole among the grass roots and its nostrils were full of the smell of field mouse. With its back to the beech tree twenty yards away, and its long nose stuck down the mousehole, it presented to Ransome the perfect target and the perfect final contemptuous gesture toward the foe. She suddenly spread her great wings and flew off her perch like an eagle, diving arrow straight at the rump of the isolated fox cub. Such were her powers of acceleration that she was traveling at almost full speed when she hit it, bowling it over and over and leaving it yelping with fright.

She turned and swept once low over the mass of

foxes, milling and yapping now in helpless fury, then climbed till the red shapes dwindled, and set course for the farm. The exercise had gone better than she had dared to hope. The fear in her mind had dwindled too.

17
The Waiting

MOST OF AUGUST HAD PASSED NOW, AND THE BLAZing, burning weather continued. The fame of the three superpullets had of course spread through the flock, and as for their present program, this was an open secret. The spirit of pride and self-reliance, of confidence and aggression, which their deeds inspired was showing itself everywhere. Though still very fearful of the dreaded long-noses and while remaining extremely wary, everyone wanted to do his or her bit; all were keen to hit back at the enemy, to face the foe bravely instead of turning tail and flying away as they had always done. As they waited, so this backs-to-the-wall, do-or-die feeling grew among the Foxearth flock in their little island fortress surrounded by the armed might of all the foxes in the sandy dells and thick woods of that piece of country.

Massey-Harris made a magnificent speech from the top of the stable clock, in which he promised that the flock would fight the long-noses in the milking parlor, in the farrowing house, in the silage pit, and on the dung heap. "We will never surrender!" he cried.

   Each day roosters and hens, cockerels and pullets, and even young growers hardly into their
adult feathers would come to the family and volun-
teer to help in some way, any way, when the invasion should come. The nine young brothers of Ransome, Sims, and Jefferies had, with their wise
mother's help, devised a ring of sentry posts guard-
ing the perimeter of the farmhouse and buildings,
and it was to man and relieve these that a special
squad of the most keen sighted of the volunteers
was sent. Icky and his eight brothers were each to
command a post, and each post was so situated
and so well manned at every daylight moment that
only in the densest fog or the most torrential rain-
storm would any fox be able to approach unseen.
No more would the long-noses have surprise as
one of their weapons. For this reason also a picked
body of the freedom fighters were formed into re-
connaissance patrols which combed every nook
and cranny of barn and shed and stack and sty
each day at dawn, in case the enemy should have
sneaked in and lain up in ambush. Nobody had
forgotten the great raid.
   Cloudless day succeeded cloudless day so that
the grass of the fields surrounding the embattled
settlement turned brown and brittle in its thirst for
rain and even surface-rooting trees like beech and
birch began to die. Everywhere the talk was of the
forthcoming invasion. Allis-Chalmers and Alfa-Laval, Bamford and Bibby, Crosfield and Claas, and
every bearer of a time-honored name within the

stout-hearted flock spoke of nothing else. Newly fledged chicks flew everywhere in excited circles, the old and the crippled came out and did what they could even if it was only to scratch up a few extra worms for the young and the strong, the patrols patrolled, the guards guarded. Massey-Harris made many more stirring speeches, and Spillers watched lovingly over the well-being of her three daughters, those magnificent flying machines who were to be in the forefront of the battle.

One day she heard a young chick who was watching the continuing daily practice (the rick sheet was almost in tatters) say to its mother, an old Dunlop who still, in her speech, clung to the local dialect, "Mother, what are those three going to do to the long-noses when they come?"

"Long-noazes?" said the old hen. "Wass mean, long-noazes? Whoy dussent carl 'em wot they be? Varxes. They'm gwaine to bust 'em, m'dear, you'll zee—they'm gwaine to bust they varxes."

And so (legend has it) the Fox Busters received their honored title.

At last came the day when the farmer decided that he had no choice but to start feeding hay to the milking herd. Many cows had dried off in preparation for autumn calving, but the milk yield of the remainder was falling, for there was no grass left in the tawny fields. He therefore picked up the thirty-two runger from its place by the nest which had satisfactorily provided his breakfast egg these last two or three weeks, carried it back to the

Dutch barn, and set it up against the stack in its former place. Fetching a tractor and trailer, he then climbed to the top of the stack and began to throw down bales to make up a load. He was careful not to disturb any sitting or brooding birds, of which there were still many.

By chance he had picked a time to move the ladder back when one of the raiders was watching the farm; and she, for it was one of the vixens, witnessed its removal. Other buildings hid it from her sharp green eyes as the farmer carried it along, but she was sure where it was going. She slipped away to tell the others.

"The ladder's back!" she panted when she reached them. "The ladder's back! Tomorrow is L-Day!"

And at the break of that next day a strange thing happened. When Spillers woke, she gave, to the astonishment of the family and her own grave embarrassment, a loud crow. But one or two of the very oldest hens, well versed in flocklore, knew that the crowing of a hen forebodes death. Whose death? they wondered.

18

The Battle of the Barnyard
(The Beginning)

CHANCE PLAYS SUCH A LARGE PART IN THE LIVES NOT only of people but also of chickens and foxes. It was the purest chance that a hen should have flown in noisy triumph from the laying of an egg at the precise moment that Farmer Farmer came out of his back door, on the day before the foxes tried their first attack on the Dutch barn nests.

From the laying of this egg followed directly these facts: that the farmer moved the ladder; that the attack was called off; that the lives of a large number of mothers and children were saved; that thus a terrible blow to the flock's morale was avoided; that the foxes were unable to make a move until the ladder was returned to its previous position; and finally that this enforced delay gave the family and the rest of the flock time to complete their training, their trials, and their preparation, in the course of which their confidence increased greatly.

From the laying of this one egg, then, it followed that when the foxes mounted their second ladder attack, they faced a very unexpected situation. The fowls still knew nothing of the threat posed by the ladder, but the foxes knew nothing of the threat posed by the fowls.

Thus the very next morning, when the foxes lay in Indian file behind the big plant of yellow rag-wort, waiting for the farmer to come out of the milking parlor, they little thought that they had already been sighted from two of the nine sentry posts, and took no notice of the silent flight of a cockerel—it was Icky—from a tree at the edge of the yard toward the main buildings.

It had been agreed that there should be no outcry when the enemy was first sighted but that they should be allowed to come in, hopefully to a spot of the flock's own choosing, before battle was joined.

After the consultation which had followed the previous odd raid, scouts had been sent out to try to trace the route by which the foxes had come; this they did easily by following a trail of molted red hairs which the raiders had shed in their state of tense excitement; so that all knew about the blind hedge and the dry ditch and the drain hole and the narrow passage. Supposing that the long-noses took the same approach (and here the fowls were gambling, for a gamble may have to be taken in even the best-laid battle plan), it was decided that at the peak moment of surprise from the raiders' point of view—that is to say, at the instant that they burst out into the yard—every available bird should fly at them, as near as they dared and with the maximum of noise. By this means they hoped to do three things: to alert the farmer and his dogs, to confuse and perhaps dismay the foxes, and to split the raiders up so as to provide individual targets for high-speed attacks by the three dauntless dive-bombers.

At Icky's warning, a troop of specially detailed young cockerel scouts and pullet guides carried the news quickly and quietly to every combatant, and all took up their positions. Two sentries remained at each sentry post in case the route of approach should be altered, while the others, including the post commanders, flew in to join the main body. Spillers and Massey-Harris went to their command post on the very top of the grain silo, the highest building of all. And on the ridgepole of the great barn sat the three sisters, the day's eggs not yet laid; they were at the very peak of condition, superbly trained, poised for instant takeoff. Around the yard, the roofs were black with grim, determined birds. All was silent.

The stillness was broken by the stable clock chiming the hour of nine, and a few moments later the farmer came out of the milking parlor into the bright sunlight of a day that was already hot and, followed by his dogs, made his way to the farmhouse. A minute later, one of the two remaining sentries on Icky's post flew in to report that the foxes were on the move, and his companion followed shortly afterward, going directly to the command post from which, almost immediately, Massey-Harris gave one loud crow. This was the prearranged signal, known to all, that the foxes had reached the narrow passage. All was ready.

19
The Battle of the Barnyard
(The End)

AT THE INSTANT WHEN THE FOXES BROKE FROM cover, while they were still in the act of turning to face the ladder, the air above and around them became thick with swooping, diving, flapping fowls, dozens and dozens of them, all yelling at the tops of their voices what had been a warning and was now a battle cry.

"Long-long-long-nose! Long-long-long-nose! Long-long-long-long-long-nose!" they screamed, and the incredibly deafening din brought Farmer Farmer running from his breakfast table, his mouth still full, his dogs at his heels, his gun in his hand.

The foxes, completely surprised by the confusion of noise and beating wings, and by the pecks and scratches which some of the boldest birds delivered as they swooped over them, leapt and twirled and stood upon their hind legs to snarl and snap and chop at their attackers.

Several of the flock fell into the dust of the yard to kick and choke and flap their last, but still a great cloud of them shouted and beat their wings in the very faces of the raiders, penning them together not far from the mouth of the passage.

After perhaps a minute of this pandemonium, one of the foxes suddenly broke free and, leaving the others to fight the fowls, sprinted for the foot of the thirty-two-runged ladder. He, for it was one of the dog foxes, reached it and began, neatly, nimbly, to climb, those hours of practice in the old rat-ridden shed showing value at last.

In the five seconds that it took him to reach halfway, the watchers at the command post realized with a cold thrill of horror, first, that foxes could climb ladders and second, that the mothers and babies on the top of the hay bales were in terrible, mortal danger. But even as they watched, dumbstruck, they saw a shape launch itself from the roof of the barn and cut down on flashing wings toward the fox, now only three rungs from the top.

They saw the pullet, Sims, bank sharply and release her egg with maximum velocity; and then suddenly, dramatically, just as his head reached the level of the top of the stack, the long-nose threw up his paws, somersaulted backward off the ladder, and crashed to the floor of the yard.

Sims had in fact judged her run quite perfectly, and an instant after she had swept over the back of the climbing fox, her egg had taken him full in the ribs, an egg as hard as a granite pebble from the seashore, an egg which, when they later found and examined it, had not even a hairline crack upon its smooth brown surface. The greenhouse and the grit had done their work. Before the fox could recover senses dazed by the blow and by the heavy fall, his prostrate shape disappeared beneath a cloud of fowls, a picked bunch of big hook-beaked, sharp-spurred roosters which Massey-Harris had kept in reserve for just such a moment. And so, beneath their tearing, pecking, slashing fury, the first fox died.

By now the second of the four raiders, a vixen, had broken free of the harassing ring. In the general scrimmage she had seen nothing of the fate of her brother; and she, too, dashed for the foot of the ladder.

Jefferies was already airborne, hovering forty feet above the roof of the Dutch barn, and as the vixen began to climb, Jefferies swooped vertically down upon her so that it seemed to the watchers that the two must meet head on. At the last instant the pullet leveled off, and they could see her beak open in the triumph shout "Egg gone!"

Simultaneously her missile struck the climbing vixen full on that long nose that was for the flock the symbol of all they hated most about their enemies; the beast lost her footing and cartwheeled away to the ground, to rise, stagger, and fall again beneath the bloodstained beaks and talons of the mob.

Bird after bird flew from all points to join in the frenzied jabbing and ripping over the two fallen enemies in a mad lust for revenge, a revenge not simply for the massacre in the fruit pen but for all the dead who had fallen, over the years.

At last even the harassing ring left the two remaining foxes and flew to join the avengers. Panting and disheveled, uncertain of what had happened and of what to do, brother and sister stood in the middle of the yard, ears flat back, lips wrinkled away from long canine teeth. After a moment of indecision, the vixen began to slink away toward the lower yard, but her brother still remained, a solitary figure in the center of the barnyard,

snarling fiercely in anger and fear and frustration as he watched the mob swarm over the bodies of the fallen.

For Spillers on the command post, this was a vital moment. The battle was half won, but the troops were out of control. How could she redirect the avenging flock? And if she could, should she set them at the dog fox and thus perhaps allow the vixen, already slinking past the great stone trough, to make good her escape? Or could she somehow split them into two bodies to attack both enemies? For a moment, good general as she was, she knew something like panic in her indecision. But her fellow general was in no doubt of the proper, the only, course to take.

Watching his daughters' deeds of daring, seeing the fall of the first two foxes, hearing the screeching, squalling scrimmage at the foot of the Dutch barn, Massey-Harris felt the blood of his jungle ancestors boil in his veins. A bluff and hearty fellow he might always have been, fond of the sound of his own loud voice, and not the most tactful of the flock, but the one thing he did not lack was courage. Now, at the sight of this solitary hated long-nose still defiant in the middle of *his* barnyard, he knew there was only one thing to do. On the top of the tall grain silo, he raised himself to his full height, spread wide his wings, threw back his head, and crowed his battle cry.

"View-halloo-halloo!" he cried and, before Spillers could make a move to caution or restrain him, hurled himself into the air and beat downward with all his strength and speed, straight at the dog fox.

Before the enemy could move, Massey-Harris was upon him, seeming with raised ruff and spread wings to be twice his normal size, his claws tight in the pelt of the snapping beast, his great beak stabbing, stabbing.

As every bird turned to watch this heroic single combat, Farmer Farmer poked his gun around the corner of the milking parlor and seeing, as he thought, a fox attacking one of his roosters, loosed off both barrels at the pair. The fox fell instantly dead, and across his body dropped the broken form of the gallant general. Massey-Harris raised his head once, seeming to look up toward his wife high upon the silo, and his beak opened, slowly. But no sound came, the head sank, and the eyes shut forever.

At the sound of the gun, every bird that could fly

took to the air, and as they rose above the buildings, they saw the one survivor, the remaining vixen, running away as hard as she could go toward the woods.

It was victory, a wonderful victory in the battle of the barnyard, but it was not yet complete. Now it was, for the second and last time in her long life, that Spillers gave a loud, loud crow. "Follow! Follow! Follow!" was her forecast of death yet to come, and as the puzzled farmer stood and scratched his head, she swept proudly down over the body of her mate, and up and away on the trail of the last enemy, while the air over Foxearth Farm emptied as the flock followed.

The vixen was running for her life. Pride and confidence had first turned to confusion and doubt, but now the only emotion left was fear. She knew that she must reach the shelter of the woods to escape the great armada of fowls that pursued her, and, belly to ground, she galloped for the trees. A quick glance over her shoulder reassured her; it looked as though the start she had would be enough, for they did not seem to be gaining on her; but at a second glance she suddenly saw the flock split in the middle and a single bird come dashing through them at undreamed-of speed. Desperately the vixen set herself to cover the last twenty yards to safety.

Ransome, watching the success in battle of her two sisters, had been confident that her turn would come to play that final decisive part for which she

had so long felt she was destined. As soon as she saw the surviving vixen beginning to slink away, she took off from the roof of the barn and climbed steeply to gain as much height as possible. She was still climbing when she heard the shotgun's roar and saw, with her sharp eyes, the death of her brave father, but she did not falter. Rather was she filled with a cold grim implacable determination, as she swung into a sharp-angled dive from five hundred feet.

The main body of the flock was already halfway down the field, but the impetus which the extra altitude lent to her own great powers of speed meant that she was traveling far faster than they. She screamed at them to let her through, and as they peeled to either side like waves before the sharp bows of a destroyer, she shot through them, faster and faster, lower and lower, gaining upon the galloping fox with every wingbeat.

Not five yards from the edge of the woods, the two shapes, one dull brown, one dark red, seemed to the pursuing flock to merge for an instant before the brown one hurled itself up in a wild climb, almost brushing the boundary trees, and the red one lay kicking in the grass.

By the time the Foxearth fowls reached the scene, the red shape lay still, and as they alighted and stood in a great circle about it, they could see that the back of its head had been broken by a hard, hard object. Flanked by her sons, Spillers looked in silence at the dead fox.

"Wouldn't Father have been proud," said Icky, standing at her right wing, and his eight bold brothers echoed, "Proud! Proud! Proud!"

At last Spillers spoke.

"Look," she said, to the family and the flock, "look up there."

High above them the brown shape had been joined by two others. As the three brown shapes flew in line abreast over the watchers, each right wing dropped, each left wing lifted, and over they went together in the victory roll.

All the four foxes were busted.

Whether there were sharp eyes watching this final extraordinary scene from the cover of the woods, or whether there were sharp noses that discovered the body in the field and the three other corpses flung on the dung heap, or whether there were sharp ears that heard the news shouted in triumph by all the roosters of the flock, I do not know. But I do know that from that day forward, there was perfect peace at Foxearth Farm.

Never again did the early patrols search the buildings, never again were the sentry posts manned, never again was the greenhouse entered, never again was heard the cry "Long-long-long-nose!"

Ransome the ringleader, and serious Sims, and jocular Jefferies, and the widow Spillers, and Icky and his eight brothers, and all the rest of that fabulous flying flock, lived on and prospered without ever again setting eyes on one single chicken-lover from the sandy dells and thick woods of that piece of country.

PATRICIA REILLY GIFF

writes about girls and boys just like you:

● clever ● cheerful ● stubborn ● mad ● brainy ● average ● happy ● sad

__THE FOURTH-GRADE CELEBITY	42676-6	$2.95
__THE GIFT OF THE PIRATE QUEEN	43046-1	$2.95
__THE GIRL WHO KNEW IT ALL	42855-6	$2.95
__HAVE YOU SEEN HYACINTH MACAW?	43450-5	$2.75
__LEFT-HANDED SHORTSTOP	44672-4	$2.75
__LORETTA P. SWEENY, WHERE ARE YOU?	44926-X	$2.75
__LOVE, FROM THE FIFTH-GRADE CELEBRITY	44948-0	$2.75
__RAT TEETH	47457-4	$2.75
__THE WINTER WORM BUSINESS	49259-9	$2.75

At your local bookstore or use this handy page for ordering:

DELL READERS SERVICE, DEPT. DPG3
P.O. Box 5057, Des Plaines, IL. 60017-5057

Please send me the above title(s). I am enclosing $_____.
(Please add $2.00 per order to cover shipping and handling.) Send check or
money order—no cash or C.O.D.s please.

Ms./Mrs./Mr._____

Address _____

City/State _____ Zip _____

DPG3–1/90

Prices and availability subject to change without notice. Please allow four to six weeks for delivery.

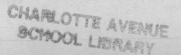